Santa's Stray in
All is Bright

Written by Polly Basore

Illustrated by Carlene H. Williams

Polly Basore

For Madison

Find the
opportunity for
goodness!

2006

Were it not for the kindness of some children in Simon's neighborhood, the black and white stray and the others might not have survived. Though it was not yet winter by the calendar, winds blew from the north, bringing an icy chill that left driveways and sidewalks slick with frost and the neighborhood creek frozen over.

But in this neighborhood, where garage doors are left open to shelter strays, outdoor pet bowls are checked frequently so that ice may be replaced with water, and cats may drink.

We speak of cats, because cats are generally allowed to roam free. It is not so with stray dogs, who can expect to be snatched from the streets and taken away to no place good. Because of this, Simon had not encountered a stray dog in his neighborhood — until this day, when he observed a small brown dog wandering anxiously down the street.

The dog seemed hurried, but with no place to go. He appeared to be looking for something, even as he tried to avoid being seen. Simon crouched low under a bush as he watched the dog find his way to a porch where a young boy had set out a bowl of water.

Steam rose from the bowl, its heat being absorbed into the cold air. The young dog could not contain his thirst and lapped it up loudly, so loudly that he did not notice a boy come to a window to watch. But as the boy made a move to open his front door, the small dog scampered off the porch and out of sight.

In the days that followed, the boy kept the water bowl filled and the dog returned again and again to drink. He even ate cat food from the bowl set beside it. Simon didn't mind because he could see that the dog was quite young and obviously hungry.

The fierce cold lasted more than a week, bringing ice, hard-packed snow and bitterly cold winds. Strays huddled in garages while the humans stayed in their houses, emerging only to go to and from their cars, and to tend the water and food bowls.

Simon wanted to invite the dog to share his garage, but the dog never gave him a chance; he stayed hidden. Simon hoped it was some place warm.

Just as it seemed the neighborhood would be cold and dark forever, Simon felt the sun begin to break through the gray. Sunshine warmed his fur and a smile of relief spread between his whiskers.

From the houses came a *drip, drip, drip* as ice melted from roof tops and tree tops. And soon, the people came out of their houses and into their yards.

What were they doing?

Simon watched curiously and tried to figure it out. He scampered up his tree to get a better view. And this is what he saw...

At the house on the
corner, an elderly woman
came out carrying green
wreaths with bright red bows.
She hung one wreath on the
front door and the others
on each of the front windows.
She carefully tied a red bow
to the mailbox. And inside,
she placed a lighted candle
in each windowsill so when
seen from outside a candle
shone through each wreath.

At the next house, a
young couple took turns
climbing a ladder to hang
white lights along the edge
of their roof. They hung
more lights on a pine tree
in the front yard, and
smiled and kissed when they
finished.

Two doors down, a man sat in his front yard untangling electric cords. He called out to his daughter to bring boxes. The girl brought box after box from the garage. The man worked for hours and when he was done, his yard was a brightly lit hodge-podge of colored lights and inflatable Santas and snowmen and lighted candy canes and reindeer.

And at the house where there is always water for the strays, Simon watched the boy who lives there help his mother carefully unpack a string of simple, old blue lights. The boy then held a ladder as the mother placed the blue lights around the front door and the front windows. Simon marveled at the lights. He thought their blue glow was the prettiest of all.

By twilight, the decorating was finished and people were back inside their houses. Simon realized what had happened: The icy cold had kept people from decorating for the holidays until now. A good thing it warmed up, Simon thought because it was surely almost Christmas. Simon fell asleep, thinking it was all so beautiful and dreaming someone had decorated his tree.

He was not asleep for long.

Grr-uff! Ruf-ruf-ruf! Grr-ruff! Ruf-ruf-ruf!

Simon woke up and looked down. He could not believe what he saw: The stray dog who never made a sound was now barking loudly, as if to sound an alarm.

It was hard for Simon to make out what was happening. The dog was barking at the house of the boy who put out food and water for strays, but that house was now dark. The blue lights the boy put up with his mother were gone.

Simon leapt from his tree and ran toward the porch in time to see a man trying to shake a dog loose from his leg. The dog would not let go. He held tight, grasping the man's pant leg with his teeth even as the man kicked. When the man's foot hit the dog's jaw, the dog finally let go and the man ran for the shadows and disappeared.

Simon wished very much at the moment that he spoke "dog," but he did not.

He watched sympathetically as the boy and his mother came out to the porch. They had heard the noise but stayed inside out of fear. Now they saw the lights gone and the young dog, shaking. The boy scooped the dog into his arms and sat with him crying, but not for long because his mother who was also upset and really not sure what to do, said, "It's late. Go inside. We should go to bed."

Simon wasn't sure what to do either, but he knew he wanted to help. The stray cat's heart ached for the boy and the dog. He wondered why something bad like this could happen to them. The boy was such a good boy; the dog was such a kind dog. They didn't deserve this. Simon wanted to understand but he couldn't. And he wanted to fix things, but he couldn't.

Who could?

Santa?

Simon scrambled back up his tree, heading for the highest branches.
The stray had managed to summon Santa Claus once before by yowling
at the North Star. Santa had told Simon when they first met that he
wanted to know when children were lonely or frightened or sad. Surely,
Santa would want to know about this!

Breo-owwwwwww! Bre-owwwwww! Simon howled at the North Star as the curious brown dog came over to the tree to watch from below. As he had done once before, Simon meowed through the night, *bre-owing* out his call to Santa until exhaustion took over and he fell asleep. The dog, somewhat fearful from all that had happened, tried hard to stay awake. But eventually he, too, went to his hiding place and fell asleep.

Night had given way to day by the time Simon's ears perked. He thought he heard a faint sound of jingle bells. The sound was too faint to wake him, though. A moment later his nose twitched. Did he smell... gingerbread? He next realized he felt warm, warmer than he had in weeks. Someone was holding him close, stroking his black and white fur ever so gently. Simon's heart leapt with excitement and he finally opened his eyes.

"Santa?!"

Simon lifted his head and looked into the eyes of an old woman. They were perhaps the kindest eyes he'd ever seen, a grayish blue with a gentle sparkle that matched her smile.

"No my dear, Santa is busy today. It's Christmas Eve!" the woman said.

Her hair was grayish white. A few strands hung loose, caked with just a bit of flour. She smelled of gingerbread. She wore a red snowsuit with a leopard-print fur trim that matched the trim on her snow boots.

"Are you Mrs. Santa?" Simon asked.

She smiled at him. "Yes, Simon. Santa is my husband, but why don't you just call me by my first name, Merry."

"Mary? Like the mother of Jesus?" asked Simon.

"No, Merry. Like Christmas ... But some of the elves call me Mother Merry," she said as she tickled the cats ears. "Now why don't you tell me what the trouble is."

Simon told Merry about the icy cold and the stray dog who came looking for water, and the boy who provided it. He told how the warm weather brought people out of their houses to decorate, how Simon thought the blue lights were the prettiest of all, and how those were the ones the thief stole. He told how the young dog, usually so careful never to be seen, came out of the shadows to try to stop the thief, but got kicked instead. And how sad this made the boy whose blue lights were stolen, the same boy who gave the dog water, and how his mother didn't know what to do.

"I thought maybe Santa could help," said Simon, tilting his head at Merry.

Merry smiled at the cat but said nothing. Instead she put the cat down, pulled a gingerbread cookie from her pocket and crouched down, holding out the treat. Her eyes scanned the neighborhood until she saw him: The dog peeked out from under the porch of the house with missing lights.

"Here boy, come here. It's all right... come here..." Merry called out, as Simon watched.

The dog cautiously approached her, asking Merry, "Is that really for me?"
Simon heard only soft barking, but Merry who like her husband knows
many animal languages, understood every word.

The dog munched the cookie from Merry's hand, which told the wise old woman that his jaw was okay. She asked the dog his name. The dog looked embarassed and said, "No one ever gave me one."

"That's too bad. Everyone should have a name," Merry said.

The dog then preceded to tell the same story about what had happened, only he added the curious description of how the black and white cat climbed a tree and began yowling into the night. "To be honest it was a horrible sound," said the dog, who felt bad for saying it but couldn't help himself.

Merry laughed. "Yes, I know. I heard it. We both did, Santa and I. All the way to the North Pole! But what is it exactly you think Santa could do about this?" Merry said, turning to Simon. Simon admitted he didn't know exactly, but he wondered if somehow Santa could get back the blue lights and decorate the house?

"Well maybe he could..." said Merry. "But he's awfully busy tonight, and I am not sure it would even be necessary."

"Why not?" asked the dog, who hung his head in disappointment.

"From what you both have told me," Merry said, "there are some very good people in this neighborhood. And when bad things happen, very good people have a way of taking care of their neighbors."

"What do you mean?" asked Simon.

"Just wait and see," smiled Merry. And with that, Simon heard a tinkling of jingle bells and Merry was suddenly gone. The cat asked the dog to come sit with him at the bottom of the tree, and there they snuggled together to see what might happen.

The young couple came out of their house first. They took down the white lights from their pine tree and brought the lights and ladder to the boy's house. They had just started hanging the strand of white lights along the boy's roof when the elderly woman came over with the wreath from her door. She hung it on the boy's door, instead.

Another neighbor came next, carrying a fist full of extension cords and dragging an inflatable Santa. He placed it in the front yard while his daughter put plastic lighted candy canes along the driveway. Soon the little house was brightly decorated again. The little boy and his mother were so happy. They invited the neighbors to come back later to see their work. The boy hugged each of them while his mother served hot cocoa.

Watching this, Simon realized that even though the family had suffered something bad, the good that happened afterward was much greater.

Was it always this way, Simon wondered? Is every bad thing that happens really just an opportunity for someone to respond with greater goodness?

Simon didn't know for sure. But he went to sleep that Christmas Eve night feeling less lonely, less afraid, and rather certain that whatever bad exists, it would be no match for good in his neighborhood.

The End

Polly Basore is founder of AngelWorks, a philanthropy committed to providing comfort and opportunity to those affected by poverty, homelessness, addiction or grief. This is her third book about the stray cat named Simon, produced with Carlene H. Williams. She is also author of a memoir, "What Heaven Left Behind," which tells the story of her personal experience with grief and how it lead to the creation of AngelWorks. Polly lives in Bel Aire, Kansas, with her son Henry and their six cats.

Carlene H. Williams is a freelance illustrator, art teacher, and designer. She holds a BFA in illustration from Brigham Young University. In addition to the Simon series, she collaborated with her father Roy E. Howard, on a bilingual book called "How Music Came to Earth." She and her husband Lucas, live in Wichita, Kansas. They are expecting their first child.

The proceeds from this book benefit **The Lord's Diner**, a soup kitchen that provides a free dinner to anyone in need 365 days a year in downtown Wichita. The Diner is made possible by the generous support of its community and its 6,000 volunteers.